Ben and Gran

and the

Whole

Wide

Wonderful

World

For Babby ~ K.M.

For Gabriel and his grandmothers ~ G.S.

First published in paperback in 2005
First published in 2004 by Macmillan Children's Books
a division of Macmillan Publishers Limited
20 New Wharf Road, London N1 9RR
Basingstoke and Oxford
Associated companies worldwide
www.panmacmillan.com

ISBN 1 405 00907 1

1 3 5 7 9 8 6 4 2

A CIP catalogue record for this book is available from the British Library.

Printed in Belgium by Proost

GILLIAN SHIELDS

Ben and Gran and the Whole Wide Wonderful World

Illustrated by Katharine McEwen

MACMILLAN CHILDREN'S BOOKS

Ben's favourite
person in the whole
wide world was Gran.

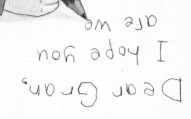

And Gran's favourite
person was Ben.

There was only one problem.

Ben's house, which was
little and red, with a slopey
roof and a rabbit in the
garden, was over here.

And Gran's house, which
was tall and twisty, and
cluttered with books and cats
and knitting, was over there.

Miles and miles and miles away.

So Gran sent letters and sweaters and boxes
of home-made fudge, miles and miles and miles,
to Ben's little red house over here.

And Ben sent Gran pictures and postcards
and holiday snaps, miles and miles and miles,
to Gran's tall twisty house over there.

Sending stuff was fun!

HELLO

Ben and Gran found lots of ways to send messages and presents.

To Ben.

But it wasn't as much fun as actually
seeing your favourite person.

So Gran sent Ben a special letter.

My dear Ben,

   I must see you, even if i have to cross the whole, wide world to do so.

   It will probably take me a week.

   Expect to see me next Saturday just before tea-time.

   Love from Gran.

   x x x

"**Yippee!**" cried Ben.

Mum helped Ben send a special email to Gran:
"See you on Saturday at tea-time!"

Then Ben thought for a bit.
"I've got a lot to do, to get ready for Gran,"
he said. "It will probably take me a week."
So he set to work.

The next day was Sunday.
Gran packed her bags.

She packed:

one umbrella

two sensible
cardigans

three red silk
petticoats

four fancy hats

five cats

six picnic lunches

and seven large maps, in case she got lost.

And Ben cut up lots
of coloured paper in
the little red house.

On Monday,
Gran set off from
her tall twisty house.
She hitched a lift on
a wagon, rode through
the forest and crossed
a rushing, rocky
river, on her way
to see Ben.

Just then, in the little red house,
Ben found an old sheet.

"Can I have this for something
special?" he asked Mum.

On Tuesday, Gran climbed a mountain,
skied down the other side and skated across
a frozen lake, on her way to see Ben.

And Ben glued and
stuck and sploshed in
the little red house.

On Wednesday,
Gran flew an
aeroplane, parachuted
down to land and crossed
the desert on a camel,
on her way to see Ben.

The camel wasn't very helpful. Gran didn't get very far that day.

But in the little red house, Ben got out his best paints and made rainbows.

On
Thursday,
Gran jumped from
a motorbike onto a motorboat
and zoomed across the shining sea,
on her way to see Ben.

The cats were all seasick, so Gran had to row.

It was a long, long way.

Back in the kitchen of the
little red house,
Ben made a
delicious,
sticky mess.

On Friday, Gran said,
"We must be there tomorrow!
Ben is expecting us!"

She studied the maps carefully.
Then she caught a tram, a bus, a subway,
a taxi and a high-speed express train,
on her way to see Ben.

At last, in the little red house,
Ben had finished being busy.
He was ready for Gran.

So he went to bed.

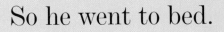

On Saturday, Gran walked and walked,
on her way to see Ben.

And Ben looked out of the window of the little
red house, and waited and waited for Gran.

Gran walked and walked.
Ben waited and waited.

Then finally, just before tea-time, Gran walked up to the front door of the little red house and called out ...

I ❤ LOVE

And Gran wasn't over there any more, miles and miles and miles and miles away, but she really was over here, with Ben.

GRaN

And Ben thought that
the little red house, with the
rabbit and the cats and Gran
at the tea table . . .

... was the best place to be

in the whole, wide, wonderful world.